Published by Sweet Cherry Publishing Limited
Unit 36, Vulcan House,
Vulcan Road,
Leicester, LE5 3EF,
United Kingdom

First published in the UK in 2018
2018 edition

ISBN: 978-1-78226-373-9

Text by Geronimo Stilton
Art Director: Iacopo Bruno
Graphic Designer: Laura Dal Maso / theWorldofDOT
Original cover illustration by Roberto Ronchi and Christian Aliprandi
Concept of illustration by Roberta Bianchi, produced by Danilo Barozzi, Carolina Livio and
Christian Aliprandi with assistance from Lara Martinelli
Initial and final page illustrations by Roberto Ronchi and Ennio Bufi MAD5, Studio Parlapà and
Andrea Cavallini. Map illustrations by Andrea Da Rold and Andrea Cavallini
Cover layout and typography by Elena Distefano
Interior layout and typography by Rhiannon Izard, Kellie Jones, Chris Ogle and Amy Wong
Graphics by Chiara Cebraro
© 2012 Edizioni Piemme S.p.A., Palazzo Mondadori – Via Mondadori, 1 – 20090 Segrate
© 2018 English edition, Sweet Cherry Publishing
International Rights © Atlantyca S.p.A. – Via Leopardi 8, 20123 Milano, Italy
Translation © 2014, Edizioni Piemme S.p.A.

Original title: *La gara dei supercuochi*
Based on an original idea by Elisabetta Dami

www.geronimostilton.com/uk

www.sweetcherrypublishing.com

Printed and bound in Turkey

WELCOME TO THE WORLD
OF
Geronimo Stilton

Geronimo Stilton

THE
SUPER CHEF
CONTEST

Sweet Cherry
Publishing

BANG, BANG, BANG ...
BANG!

It was a beautiful morning. The first rays of the sun peeked through my curtains, warming the blankets on my cosy bed. I was tucked in peacefully, the covers pulled up, snoring like a hibernating dormouse.

Oops! I always forget to introduce myself: my name is Stilton, *Geronimo Stilton*. I'm the editor of The

Rodent's Gazette, the most famouse newspaper on Mouse Island.

Anyway, I was dreaming of biting into my favourite breakfast treat (a cheese-filled doughnut with vanilla frosting) when suddenly I heard a deafening sound outside. What was that terrible noise? It sounded more or less like this:

BANG, BANG, BANG ... BANG!!!

I jumped out of bed with a squeak. Then I threw open the window and something wet, mushy, and smelly hit me right in the snout. **SPLAT!**

Ugh! I spat out the soggy substance, which had a strange odour. What could it be?

"AAARRRGGGH!" I squeaked. "Who's there? What was that?"

Then I heard a familiar voice: "Cousin!" the voice boomed. "Do you care about me or not?"

Only then did I understand ...

That maybe ...

No, probably...

No, surely it was ...

Cousin!

my cousin Trap Stilton!

"So, did you like it?" Trap yelled loudly.

"Wh-what was I supposed to like?" I sputtered in response. "I don't understand!"

As I was squeaking, Trap used a small wind-up catapult to shoot another smelly brown glob at me. It landed right in my mouth.

I spat it out. It tasted *disgusting*.

"No!" I yelled. "I don't like it! But what is it?"

"It's a liver-flavoured, deep-fried, Cheddar cheese meatball!" he announced proudly.

Then he began to interrogate me. "Why don't you like it? What would you change? Is it too sweet or too salty or too spicy or too bland or too dense or too soft or too –"

"STOP!" I yelled, cutting him off. "I just don't like it, and that's that. Ugh!"

But Trap just pulled a notebook out of his pocket and began to write furiously.

"'The victim – I mean, the taster – I mean, the assistant said he doesn't like it, and that's that. *Ugh*!'"

Then he snapped shut the notebook.

"You know, Geronimo, this doesn't work for me," he said.

"What doesn't work for you?" I asked, confused.

"These tasting notes!" Trap squeaked. "You must be more precise, more complete, and go into more detail. **Otherwise, how will I improve the flavour of my dishes?**"

The assistant says ...

Raw Egg Smoothie (Shells Included!)

I watched from my window as Trap dashed inside the **ENORMOUSE** two-storey white camper he had parked on my front lawn. Suddenly, he popped up through the roof of the camper van and jumped towards me, flying through my open window. He landed on the floor of my bedroom. I was flabbergasted.

"B-but ... the camper van ... the window ..." I squeaked, unable to complete a sentence. Then Trap stuffed a slice of cake into my snout.

"Wild onion cake with cherry cream cheese frosting," he announced proudly.

BLECH! It was awful! It tasted like rancid rubbish! I spat it out, disgusted.

"Here, Cuz!" Trap said, handing me a cup filled with a murky-looking liquid. "Wash it down with this!"

RAW EGG SMOOTHIE (SHELLS INCLUDED)!

Blech! It was dreadful! It tasted like a raw egg smoothie, with the shells included.

I spat out the drink.

"This isn't going well, Geronimo," Trap said, shaking his snout. "You must give me more constructive feedback, understand? Otherwise, how will I win the Super Chef Contest and become the recipient of the **Great Golden Fork**?"

Then Trap reached over and tweaked my ear. **Ouch!**

"What are you squeaking about?" I asked. Then I remembered an article I had published a few days earlier in The Rodent's Gazette. "Do you mean the upcoming Super Chef

This isn't going well ...

WILD ONION CAKE WITH CHERRY CREAM CHEESE FROSTING!

Contest in Gourmetville, which determines the best cook on Mouse Island?" I asked Trap.

He reached over and tweaked my other ear. **Double ouch!**

"Exactly!" he replied. "And do you know who will win? Me! But there is one little teeny, tiny detail ..."

He reached over and tweaked my tail. **Triple ouch!**

"I need a victim – I mean, a taster – I mean, an assistant," Trap continued. "And it's going to be you, Cuz!"

"B-but I can't, I really can't," I stammered. "I have so much work to do at the office. And I'm not a very good cook. Why don't you ask someone else?"

Trap pointed his finger at me.

"You know, you're a really *shellfish* mouse, Geronimo," he said, poking me in the snout. Unfortunately for me,

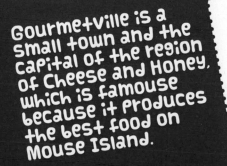

Gourmetville is a small town and the capital of the region of Cheese and Honey, which is famouse because it produces the best food on Mouse Island.

Geronimo Stilton

he missed his target and poked me in the eye instead.

"Owwwwww!" I yelped with pain.

"Ha, ha, ha!" Trap laughed, oblivious. "Did you get my little chef pun, Cuz? *Shellfish!*

You're really shellfish!

OWWWWWW!

"Anyway," Trap continued, "it's got to be you. I asked Thea, but she can't because she has to accompany Aunt Sweetfur to a crochet class. I asked Coral Cockle, but she can't because she's waiting for a delivery of mussels from the Sea of Mice. I asked my friend Paws Prankster,

I can't ...

CORAL COCKLE

16

but he can't because he's **allergic** to every food except cheese and spinach. I also asked my friend Fishyfur, but he can't because he's having a birthday party for his pet fish Red.

PAWS PRANKSTER

"I asked Tootsie from the Telltail Tavern, and he won't do it because a month ago we had a fight (in which I was right, naturally!). I even asked my friends Squeaky La Rue and Henrietta Happypaws, but they can't because ... because ... well, I can't remember anymore,

FISHYFUR

TOOTSIE

SQUEAKY LA RUE

17

but they can't, you see! So now I'm asking you, Geronimo. You're my cousin, and we're family, right?"

He fell to his knees, **pleading** with me.

I can't ...

HENRIETTA HAPPYPAWS

"I care about you, Cuz, but do you care about me?" Trap asked. "If you do care, you would be my assistant. If not, admit that I don't matter to you a whisker and that all you care about is your work."

Then he began to sob.

"I'm broke, G!" he squeaked. "I spent a fortune on this supercamper, which is fitted with a top-of-the-line, professional kitchen!"

"But, Trap, who made you buy an enormouse supercamper?" I asked.

He snorted. "Well, no one, exactly, but ... well, do you care about me or not?"

I sighed. It's true that I have a heart that's as **soft** as Brie. I'd be willing to do almost anything for anymouse

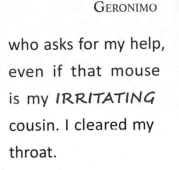

who asks for my help, even if that mouse is my *IRRITATING* cousin. I cleared my throat.

"Trap, if this is really that important to you, well, maybe I should ... I would ... well, I'll be your assistant," I agreed.

He jumped up and down with joy. Then he pulled me on board his supercamper, which was indeed fitted for a professional chef. **I looked around in shock.** There was every tool imaginable: from A to Z, apple corers to zesters! There were the most modern appliances, a library of recipes from the most famouse chefs, and many, many other things!

Trap's HUGE Supercamper

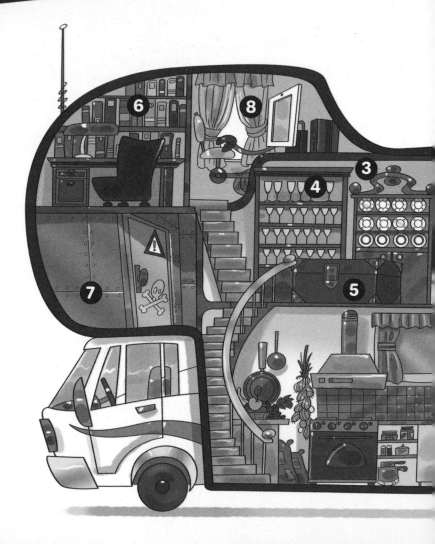

1. BEDROOM, BATHROOM, AND WALK-IN WARDROBE FURNISHED COMPLETELY FOR CHEFS
2. LARGE KITCHEN FITTED WITH A GIANT REFRIGERATOR, A FREEZER, A BEVERAGE FRIDGE, APPLIANCES, POTS, PANS, AND EVERYTHING ELSE NEEDED BY THE BEST CHEFS!
3. PLACE SETTINGS FOR TWELVE, EDGED IN GOLD FOR SPECIAL OCCASIONS
4. HAND-BLOWN CRYSTAL GLASSES
5. TRAP'S MYSTERIOUS LARGE TRUNK: WHO KNEW WHAT WAS INSIDE?
6. LIBRARY OF BOOKS AND RECIPES BY THE MOST FAMOUSE CHEFS!
7. SECRET ROOM (ONLY TRAP HAD THE KEY!)
8. TELEVISION ROOM WITH VIDEO GAMES AND COMPUTER FOR RELAXATION
9. GYM TO STAY IN SHAPE

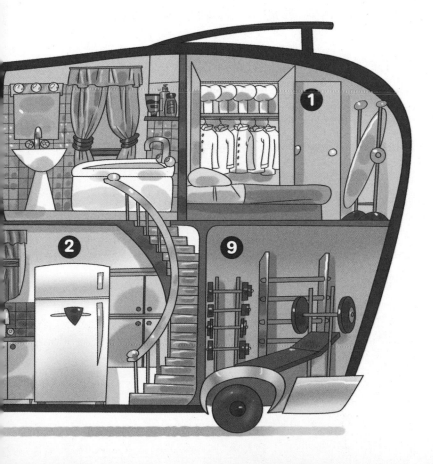

WELCOME TO GOURMETVILLE!

Trap hopped in the driver's seat and drove off in a flash, tyres squealing. And then he began to sing:

"The amazing Trap Stilton is on his way,
To cook the best dishes of the day!
He'll slice them and dice them,
He'll fry them and ice them,
And when he wins, we'll shout 'hooray'!"

Trap wouldn't stop chattering as we drove. "Don't worry, Cousin," he bragged, "this contest will be a walk in the park! The **Great Golden Fork** is already mine! And do you know why? Because I'm the best! I'm prepared! I studied all the rules of the contest. Listen ..."

Rules of the

SUPER CHEF CONTEST

The contest takes place every year in Count Ludwig von Cheddar's ancient castle in Gourmetville, in the region of Cheese and Honey. Count von Cheddar was a true gourmand who was passionate about cooking until he died many years ago from indigestion. This contest is his legacy.

Every rodent on Mouse Island is eligible to enter the contest. The contest lasts seven days. The first six days are elimination rounds. On the evening of the sixth day, the top seven participants will be selected to compete in the final competition on the seventh day.

The winner will receive the Great Golden Fork trophy, which he or she will retain until the following year's contest. In addition, the winner will receive a certificate that verifies him or her as Mouse Island's Super Chef of the Year. May the best mouse win!

I listened to him carefully. **MOULDY MOZZARELLA!** The Super Chef Contest lasted for seven days. An entire week! Yikes! **Poor me!** This meant that I would be required to assist my cousin for seven whole days ... which meant that I would have to taste yucky mush non-stop for seven whole days. I became NAUSEATED just thinking about it! Between that and the bumpy ride in the supercamper, I was beginning to worry I might throw up! Luckily, a moment later, I saw a sign that read:

MAP **OF** MOUSE ISLAND

Pirate Island

Panther Archipelago

Hamster Islands

Tomcat Island

Cat's Claw Bay

Swissville

Blue Dolphin Bay

San Mouscisco

Stray Cat Harbour

Mouseport

Trap's Supercamper

New Mouse City

Mousefort Beach

Gourmetville

Count Ludwig von Cheddar's Castle

Furflung Island

Cheese and Honey Region

We had arrived in Gourmetville, the capital of Mouse Island's Cheese and Honey region, which is famouse for producing the best food on the island. The cheeses in this city are the most delicious, the fruit is the tastiest, and the recipes are the most interesting.

I looked around: many of Gourmetville's antique buildings were decorated with elaborate plaster like frosted birthday cakes. The streets had gourmet names: Frittata Alley, Cheesecake Lane, Sweet & Salty Street, Lasagne Way ... the list went on and on! Street signs pointed the way to the Mouseum of Taste and the Mouseum of Cheeses.

And there were so many places to eat! All around me there were restaurants, cafés, pizzerias, grocery stores, delis, ice cream shops, bakeries, butchers, and candy stores.

On the main street, I spotted the offices of the local newspaper, The Gourmand Press. The editors only publish recipes, results of cooking competitions and restaurant reviews! The streets were clogged with tourists, journalists, and chefs who had come to

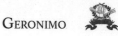

Gourmetville to attend the event of the year.

Trap turned down a narrow street that led to a small hill in the area that surrounded the city. The supercamper climbed up the hill towards a castle perched on the steep rocks overlooking Gourmetville.

It was Count von Cheddar's castle! There was a huge banner hanging over the front door:

THE
SUPER CHEF
CONTEST

I'm going to win!

So many chefs!

WHAT AN EVENT!

The line of chefs waiting to enter the castle snaked out the door and around the building not once, but twice!

Fried Snail Pie with Oyster Sauce

We got out of the camper, and Trap pulled out his mysterious, locked, red metal trunk. A sign on the trunk read: PAWS OFF!

I wondered what was inside. Hmm! But there wasn't time to ask him about it because he was already jostling to get into line.

While we waited in line, I raised my eyes towards the castle and shivered. Dim lights shone from the highest windows, giving the castle a very spooky air!

No one can resist my soufflé!

WE'LL SEE WHO WINS!

I remembered some local legends I had heard – it's said that the **ghost** of Count von Cheddar still prowls the castle at night, complaining about his indigestion.

But I didn't have time to think about it because there were lots of journalists hanging around the castle, and suddenly one recognised me.

"Aren't you Geronimo Stilton?" he asked. "Editor of The Rodent's Gazette? Are you publishing a special report on the contest?"

"Yes, I'm Geronimo Stilton," I admitted. But before I could explain that I wasn't there as a reporter, Trap

I'm the best chef around!

Future Super Chef here!

What a contest!

plugged my mouth with a piece of fried snail pie with oyster sauce.

"Don't get distracted!" Trap hissed as he tweaked my ear. "So, how would you rate this recipe, on a scale from one to ten?"

Ouch! And blech! The pie was disgusting.

"It's horrendous!" I squeaked. "I'd give it a three and a half, and that's being generous!"

But instead of being discouraged, Trap just continued to shove dishes into my mouth:

First course: A dark chocolate dumpling stuffed with pickles and dipped in strawberry sauce.

Second course: A goat's cheese tart with a spicy orange glaze.

Third course: Beans and rice with chopped cherries and mayonnaise.

Trap pinched my other ear. "So?" he asked. "On a scale of one to ten, what do you think? Eight? Nine? Or maybe ten?"

"I'd give you a negative one!" I squeaked, gagging. "All of those dishes were just AWFUL!"

Trap leaned over and tweaked my tail.

"All right, Cuz!" he said, undeterred. "That means I'll

34

try again! I'll make you taste many, many more dishes until they are perfect. Okay?"

I groaned. I felt SICK TO MY STOMACH just thinking about tasting many, many more dishes! I considered ducking out of the line and trying to escape, but I suddenly realised that we were already in the castle and at the front of the line. A bored-looking official was questioning Trap.

"First name?" the official asked, stifling a yawn. "Last name? Address? Cooking experience?"

Naturally, Trap began to brag about himself: "I am Trap Stilton, the **best** cook on Mouse Island. I'm a real expert. I mean, I understand food, you know? I'm the next winner of the Super Chef Contest, just wait and see!"

The official snorted.

"That's what they all say," he grumbled. "If you really are the best, we'll all know soon enough. In the meantime, sign here."

He handed a sheet of paper to Trap, then assigned him a name tag in the form of a chef's hat that said:

Contestant Chef Number 117.

The official interviewed me next. Then he pinned a name tag on my chest that read: **Contestant Chef Number 117's Assistant**. Trap grabbed a marker and crossed out

Assistant and wrote **Victim**. Then he changed his mind and crossed it out again, writing **Taster** instead.

A moment later, a mouse with a megaphone made an announcement. **"Ahem!"** He cleared his throat. "Attention, contestants! Tonight you and your assistants will sleep in the rooms you have been

assigned. The contest will begin tomorrow at 9 a.m. sharp, in the castle's kitchen."

With a sigh, I followed Trap down a dark, dismal corridor towards the room we were assigned to share. Torches on the walls cast super-spooky shadows.

I shuddered with fright. Who knew if the ghost of Count von Cheddar would appear that night? Yikes!

I noted that Trap also seemed to be in a hurry to get to our room. **How strange!** He ran through the corridor, dragging the large red metal trunk behind him. How very strange! Come to think of it, I was surprised he hadn't made me drag his trunk for him. **How very, very strange!**

Cobwebs, Vintage Cheddar, and Ancient Stains!

There were two canopy beds in our room. Each bed had red curtains and a gold chef's hat on top. They were also covered in authentic vintage cobwebs. Dusty cooking trophies lined the mantel, and an enormouse oil painting of Count Ludwig von Cheddar hung on the wall. The painting smelled like authentic vintage MUMMIFIED Cheddar. And the bedspreads, curtains, tablecloths, and canopies were all stained with food: they were authentic vintage stains!

I looked around the room, feeling anxious. What if this had been Count von Cheddar's bedroom? My whiskers trembled as I thought about the possibility of bumping into his ghost in the middle of the night.

Trap, on the other hand, didn't even seem to notice his surroundings. Instead, he rushed into the room, opened a screen in front of his bed, and pulled the red metal trunk behind it. **HOW STRANGE!**

A second later, something shot out from behind the screen. I bent down to find that it was an electric plug. **HOW VERY STRANGE!**

I stepped closer to the screen to give the plug back to Trap. Behind the screen, I saw my cousin reading an instruction manual. I made out the letters **FRE** before Trap quickly moved the screen so I couldn't see anything else. **HOW VERY, VERY STRANGE!**

An electric plug?

"Oops, sorry!" I apologised. "I didn't mean to pry."

"Well, don't peek anymore!" Trap squeaked in reply. "I'm not sharing my cooking secrets with anyone, not even you, Cuz!"

Then I heard a click, and I immediately began to hear a strange **BUZZING** sound that continued all night long. A few minutes later Trap began to snore loudly. **ZZZZZZ ...**

Between the buzzing sound from behind the screen and Trap's snoring, I didn't close my eyes all night long.

The next morning, a loud gong startled me. It was the signal for all of the chefs and their assistants to

Oops, sorry!

report to the kitchen. I dragged myself out of bed and headed straight for the mirror to comb my fur.

"**Ahhhhh!**" I squeaked, gasping with fright. It was the ghost of Count von Cheddar! Trap sat up in his bed and laughed.

"*HA, HA, HA!*" he giggled. "Scared of your own reflection?"

It was true: it wasn't a ghost in the mirror – it was me! I had such dark circles under my eyes that I hadn't recognised myself. I sighed. **It was going to be a loooong week.**

GERONIMO STILTON STINKS!

All of the chefs came out of their rooms at the same time. Trap was the only one accompanied by a victim – or rather, a taster – I mean, an **assistant**. Which is to say, me! We all headed to the kitchen, which was a cavernous room, decorated with a collection of antique copper pots.

A contest official stepped forwards, took an enormouse ladle, and banged it on an enormouse copper pot. **DIIINNNG!**

"The Super Chef Contest has begun!" he cried.

Every chef began to cook immediately. But Trap pulled out a screen from his trunk and put it in front of his stove.

"You!" he ordered me. "Victim – I mean, taster – I mean, assistant! Stand in front of this screen and

make sure no one spies on me, got it? My recipes are
TOP SECRET, understand?"

Then he pulled the red metal trunk behind the
screen, where it was out of sight.

The other chefs began to grumble.

"It's not fair!"

"Contestant Chef 117 is cheating!"

My recipes are top secret!

An official appeared at our station, followed by a
mouse pushing a cart with a giant book on top. The
book was called *Rules of the Super Chef Contest*.

"All right, all right," he called out, silencing the
contestants. "Let's take a look."

He pored over the rules silently for a looong time. Then he closed the book with a decisive **BANG!**

LET'S TAKE A LOOK ...

"There is no rule that prohibits a contestant from putting a screen in front of his or her cooking station!" he declared.

Trap peeked out from behind the screen and stuck his tongue out at everyone.

I turned bright red from the tip of my tail to the ends of my whiskers. **Why, oh why did my cousin have to be so embarrassing?**

Pfffff+!

"Ahem, excuse us," I told the other contestants sheepishly. "My cousin is, er, very nervous because of the tension of the competition."

The other chefs didn't buy it. They began to throw cabbage heads and rotten eggs at me.

To save myself, I hid inside a rubbish bin. I re-emerged at the end of the day's competition. Unfortunately for me, I was greeted by the *FLASHING* cameras of all of the photographers covering the competition. And by then, I smelled like a sewer in the hot, sticky month of August. I imagined the headlines of the newspapers the next day: GERONIMO STILTON STINKS!

"Don't worry!" Trap said. "I'll take care of it!"

Trap pulled me behind the screen.

He shoved me into a large pot.

He showered me with a bottle of water.

He dried me off with a dishrag.

He combed my fur with a fork.

Finally, he greased my whiskers with olive oil, then he dressed me as a waiter and pushed me out from behind the screen.

"Now, go serve my dishes with class, understand?" he squeaked. **"We must win!"**

WHEN TRAP IS AROUND, IT'S NEVER GOOD FOR ME!

1 Ouch!

How awful!

When Trap mocked the other cooks, they all threw rotten eggs and vegetables at me, not him!

2 Blech!

I didn't know what to do, so to save myself, I hid in the rubbish bin! How stinky!

3 Poor me!

ARE YOU GERONIMO STILTON?!

YOU STINK!

When I came out, I stank like a sewer rat, and the photographers took a ton of photos!

4

I'll take care of it!

To clean me up, Trap shoved me into a pot and showered me with bottled water.

5

What are you doing?

It's the final touch!

Then he dried me with a dishrag and combed my whiskers with a fork.

6

Huh?

Finally he dressed me like a waiter and told me to serve his dishes with class!

YUM YUM YUM YUM YUM!

For the first time, I got a glimpse of the dishes my cousin had cooked. They looked delicious, and they smelled *divine!* I licked my whiskers.

So Trap did know how to cook! Why had he made me taste all of those disgusting dishes, then? **How strange!**

But I couldn't stop to think about it because my cousin tweaked my tail and began shrieking in my ear.

Voilà!

"Come on, Geronimo, hurry up!" he squeaked.

"The judges are waiting! Don't make me look bad, I beg you. And above all, try to look like a waiter!"

Try to look like a waiter? What did that mean? I shrugged

50

and placed a napkin on my left arm, trying my best. Then I stepped forwards unsteadily, my shiny, olive oil–coated whiskers trembling nervously. How stressful!

I tried to balance all of the plates at the same time without stumbling and without spilling anything. **CREAMY CHEDDAR**, it was tough! I served the judges Trap's food and stood there silently while they crunched and munched.

The first judge was the famous Saucy Le Paws, the biggest pasta expert on Mouse Island.

The second judge was Gordon Ratsey, the most famouse celebrity

SAUCY LE PAWS

He's a pro with pasta, whether it's lasagne, tagliolini, ravioli, or spaghetti!

GORDON RATSEY

An award-winning chef who is very intimidating. Everyone is afraid of him because he's very critical and he doesn't like anything!

chef on Mouse Island. He was known for being very, very hard to please. Every time he tasted something, he said, "Ugh! Not bad, but it needed a little more salt," or "Ugh! Not bad, but it needed less butter ..."

The third judge was Julia Mouselet, author of the celebrated cookbook *The Delight of Cooking with Cheese*. She was famouse for being a tremendous chatterbox!

The fourth judge was Rodento McEgo, a very serious food critic with a waxed moustache. He always wore very elegant coat-tails and a top hat.

The four judges tasted all of the contestants' dishes in silence. After each tasting, each judge raised a scorecard with a number on it from one to ten. But none of the

RODENTO MCEGO

He's a very famouse food critic with a tiny waxed moustache and a very big ego!

contestants earned a score above a six!

HOLEY CHEESE! These judges were very tough! When it was finally Trap's turn, Saucy tasted the dishes quietly before he announced his score:

"Very tasty: I give it an eight!"

Gordon Ratsey grumbled, "Ugh! Not bad, but it needed a little more salt. Still, I give it an eight!"

Julia Mouselet consulted her famouse cookbook and **shrieked** with delight.

"This chef has executed to perfection the recipe on page thirty-three of my book," she said proudly. "I give it an eight! And he has nice whiskers, too. They remind me of my cousin's uncle's nephew Fred's ..."

She would have gone on talking for at least an hour, but Rodento McEgo leaned over and plugged her mouth with a piece of bread.

"I give it an eight!" he announced.

The host of the contest stepped up to the microphone.

"The winner of the first challenge is Contestant Chef 117: Trap Stilton of New Mouse City!" he said. "Congratulations!"

"Yes!" Trap cried out. **"I'm the best!"**

I'm the best!

PAWS OFF, MISS!

As soon as Trap stopped rejoicing, Julia Mouselet approached the screen. Her glasses were studded with rhinestones, and she had a high-pitched, dramatic squeak.

"Now that you've won, Contestant Chef 117, what's in that trunk you have hidden behind this screen?"

She tried to push the screen aside with her paw, but Trap was too quick. He poked her paw with a rolling pin.

"Not so fast!" he yelled. "Paws off, miss! Every cook has his secrets, and I have a few of my own ..."

Trap quickly closed and locked the trunk. Then he put the key on a string and hung it around his neck so that no mouse could open the trunk unexpectedly.

HOW STRANGE!

I was about to ask for an explanation when he began pushing me towards the kitchen.

"Don't try to be sly, Cousin," he said shrewdly. "I did all the cooking, so you wash the dishes!"

I stared at the stack of dishes

– *IT WAS A MILE HIGH!*

The dishes were also greasy and smelled worse than the SEWERS of New Mouse

I cooked, so you wash!

What?

56

City. What a terrible job! And while it's true that Trap had done the cooking, I hadn't even had the chance to enjoy the food!

By the time I had finished washing everything, it was late afternoon. There weren't any more challenges scheduled for the day, so I thought I'd relax a bit. I was just about to take a **Cheddar-scented bubble bath** when Trap grabbed me by the ear and dragged me to his camper van parked outside.

Once there, he insisted I taste one disgusting dish after another. Trap said he was preparing for the next day.

Yuck! Poor me!

While I swallowed each awful mouthful, I wondered how Trap had cooked such *delicious* dishes during the contest when everything he had made me taste was so terrible. Then I realised it was probably just another one of his practical jokes! Trap loves playing silly little jokes on me.

When he finally let me go, I had such a stomach ache! I had to swallow a gigantic antacid to help me

digest everything. Then I climbed into bed and tried to get some rest.

I tossed and turned for hours before I finally fell asleep. In my dreams, a portrait of Count Ludwig von Cheddar on the castle wall came to life! The count did nothing but wail and complain about having a terrible stomach ache. In the morning, I woke from my nightmare covered in sweat. I barely slept a wink!

Oh, poor, poor me!

59

Seven Chefs Remain!

For the rest of the week, the large kitchen in the castle was the site of one competition after another.

On Monday the chefs cooked *appetisers*.

On Tuesday they made first courses.

On Wednesday roasts were on the menu.

On Thursday it was fish dishes.

On Friday they made cheese.

On Saturday it was **dessert.**

Yay!

And Sunday would be the final round!

Each round, another chef was eliminated. By Saturday evening, all of the defeated chefs had left the competition with their tails between their legs.

Only seven chefs remained.

The seven best chefs on Mouse Island.

But at the end, only one would win.

That mouse would receive the **Great Golden Fork**.

He or she would be Super Chef of the Year!

The winning chef would get to appear on the hit television show **MouseChef**! And the winning chef would become famouse all over Mouse Island.

The Seven Final Chefs

1. SAMMY SUGARPAWS

He's one of the finest pastry chefs in New Mouse City.

2. BETTY BAKERMOUSE

She travels as much as she can and specialises in food from around the world.

3. RENÉE BRÛLÉE

Called 'The Sophisticated Chef', she is an expert in French haute cuisine.

4. BLAINE MCVAIN

His nickname is 'The Star' because he always brags about his dishes. He says he doesn't specialise in anything because he's the best at everything!

5. STELLA SEAWHISKERS

Her nickname is 'The Fishermouse' because she is great at fish dishes.

6. CHARLIE CUSTARD

His nickname is 'The Egg Wizard' because he specialises in egg dishes.

7. TRAP STILTON

The journalists have nicknamed him 'The Mystery Chef' because of his now famouse screen. No one knows yet what his specialties are! His assistant and taster is Geronimo Stilton.

As we watched the eliminated contestants head home, Trap chuckled under his breath. **"See you later!"** he said.

I, on the other paw, felt sorry for the chefs who had to leave. They had been up against tough competition, and I didn't like to see them go.

See you later!

On Saturday night, the remaining chefs went to their rooms early. Some reviewed recipes, some *shined* their pots and pans, and some went to bed early so they would be fresh and rested for the next day.

Sunday would be the day of the final round in the Super Chef Contest. Every contestant would have to show the judges his or her finest work. It wouldn't be easy to win the **Great Golden Fork**!

All of the chefs were very nervous that night. I offered to make everyone camomile tea. I'm a modest

mouse, but I must admit that I make a
delicious and relaxing cup of tea! Still,
the only chef who seemed calm
that night was my cousin Trap. He
hummed and whistled happily
while everyone else *trembled*
with nerves!

"Tra-la-la!" sang Trap.
"The winner is here!"

HOW STRANGE!
Why was Trap so sure
of himself when the
other chefs were all
so nervous?

Cheers!

When I offered my cousin a nice cup of camomile
tea, he brushed me aside.

"You drink it, Cuz!" he squeaked. "I don't need to. I'm
already **sooooooo relaxed**, because I'm sure I'll win!

Then he dragged his mega-trunk on wheels behind
his screen. A moment later, I again heard a familiar
buzzing sound. And then Trap began to snore, as usual.

ZZZZZZZZZZZZZZZZ!

The camomile tea I had made should have made me very sleepy, but I was wide awake. Even though I wasn't competing, I was just as anxious as the other chefs about the next day's contest!

I was sitting up in bed reading to pass the time until I was tired enough to sleep when a terrible storm struck the countryside outside my window. The summer sky lit up with flashes of lightning as thunder shook the entire castle!

A moment later, all the lights went out. Squeak!

For the Love of Cheese ...

I was finally able to fall asleep many hours later when the *THUNDER AND LIGHTNING* had stopped and the silence returned.

I woke up the next morning when my cousin's mobile phone rang. It was my aunt Sweetfur calling. She has the **LOUDEST** squeak ever, so I could hear the entire conversation clearly.

Was the soufflé good?

"So, dear, how was the party you had for your friends?" she asked Trap. "Did they like the dishes I prepared? Was the Gorgonzola soufflé good? And how about the three-cheese lasagne?"

Hmmm ... ?

Soufflé? Lasagne? Huh? **What was going on?**

"And tell me how the fondue with croutons turned out," Aunt Sweetfur continued. "Was it melted enough? And was the aubergine Parmesan cooked enough? And how was the ricotta pie? And the roast? And the cheesecake? And everything else?"

For the love of cheese, I couldn't believe my ears! **Those were the dishes Trap had cooked during the competition!**

"Thanks again, Aunt Sweetfur!" Trap replied into the phone. "Everything was delicious! My friends devoured it all! You're the best cook in New Mouse City. Bye!"

Thanks again! It was delicious!

What a scam! It sounded like Trap had cheated! But how had he done it?

Aunt Sweetfur had cooked all the dishes, but how had Trap kept them fresh? *Hmmm ... of course!* He had put them in his special trunk, which was really a portable freezer. That's why Trap had always hidden behind the screen – he didn't want anyone to see him pulling out the frozen dishes Aunt Sweetfur had prepared for him!

The plug I had seen on the night we arrived was for the freezer! And the strange **BUZZING** noise … yup, it had been the freezer!

So that's why everything my cousin cooked tasted horrible but he still won all of the competitions. During the contests, he defrosted Aunt Sweetfur's delicious dishes, while his practice dishes were what he had really made (and they were truly **DISGUSTING**, believe me!).

By now, it was very clear to me: **my cousin Trap had cheated!**

Hee, hee, hee!

I leaped out of bed and pushed Trap's screen aside.

"I can't believe it, Trap!" I squeaked. "You cheated! You tricked everyone.

Shame on you!

It's time for you to confess!"

Trap didn't look ashamed at all, though.

"But don't you think I'm a genius, Cousin?" Trap replied.

Hee, hee, hee!

"I should win the contest just for my cleverness."

I shook my head in disbelief. But before I could say anything, he threw open the freezer.

"This is the secret to how I'll win the title **Super Chef of the Year**!" he exclaimed. "Look at this beautiful food! Smell the amazing aroma!"

I looked, but the only thing I saw in the freezer was an oozing glob of green SLIME! And I smelled it, too: PEE-YOO! What a stench!

It smelled like rotten eggs, mouldy socks, and Gorgonzola with worms – combined! Blech!

The thunderstorm the previous night had caused

the castle to lose electrical power, and the freezer had been shut off, too! That meant all of the food had gone bad ... and now it was covered in a swarm of FLIES!

OUCH! I DISLOCATED MY KNEE!

Trap gasped in horror.

"*NOOOO!*" he squeaked as his snout turned pale. "What a disaster! This is a complete cat-astrophe! It's a tragedy!"

He dove towards the fridge in an attempt to save some of the food, but

Oooooops!

Help!

1

2

he slipped in the OOZING GREEN SLIME.

Then he did a flip with a twist, shouted "Help!" and crash-landed on the ground, bashing his knee! **BANG!**

A second later, he started to yell and squeak in pain: **"Ouch! Ouchie! Ow, ow, ow!** I think I dislocated my kneecap. I broke my knee! I sprained my paw! I'm in big trouble!"

And then he fainted.

I quickly revived him and then hurried to the door of the room, where I called for help. It turned out there was a doctor staying at the castle.

The doctor took one look at Trap and confirmed that my cousin really had dislocated his kneecap, broken his other knee, and sprained his paw!

I called an **ambulance**, and Trap had to be taken out of the castle on a stretcher.

As he left, some of the other chefs kindly wished him a quick recovery, but others grinned, rubbing their paws together.

"Excellent! Very good!" one chef muttered.

"That's one less chef to defeat!" another mumbled.

"This will make it easier to win!" a third chef added.

How do you feel?

GOOD LUCK!

POOR GUY!

Julia Mouselet approached the stretcher.

"Are you withdrawing from the competition, Trap?" she asked.

Trap almost leaped off the stretcher.

"*NO!*" he squeaked. "I will not withdraw! I nominate Geronimo as my replacement!"

But many of the chefs protested:

"Oh, no! *That's not fair!* Trap is the chef who entered the contest! If he goes, he is disqualified!"

A contest official frantically consulted the contest's large rule book.

"Ladies and gentlemice, the rules are very clear," he explained. "Article 737 says: 'If a contestant is forced to drop out of the contest for any reason, he or she can

nominate his or her assistant as a replacement chef.'"

"**No, no, no!**" I squeaked. "I couldn't possibly accept."

I had had enough of tasting and cooking and scrubbing pots and pans, and above all else, of my cousin's cheating!

"So you're abandoning me in my moment of need?" Trap accused me from his stretcher. "Here I am with a dislocated knee, and you're thinking only of yourself. **I didn't think you were so selfish, Cousin!**"

"But I've been helping you all week!" I protested. "I

was your victim, your taster, your assistant, and even your dishwasher! Now I would like to go home. I have so much work to do at the office, and ..."

I trailed off. Trap was blowing his nose on my tie, *sobbing* like a tiny mouselet.

Everyone around us was watching and shaking their heads.

"What a **HEARTLESS** rodent!" someone muttered.

"How could he abandon a relative like that?"

At that point, I gave in.

"Oh, all right!" I agreed. "I will compete in your place, Trap! But no more cheating! I'll compete fairly. Do you understand?"

He put his chef's hat on my head.

"Take this," he squeaked, "and compete as you wish. Just whatever you do, win! I want the **Great Golden Fork**. Work hard, and don't make me look bad!"

MOULDY MOZZARELLA! How stressful. Would I be able to do it?

SOMETHING SPECIAL – NO, SOMETHING AMAZING!

The first thing I had to do was decide on the menu. What could I prepare for the final contest that night? It had to be something simple but delicious, traditional but original, filling but light. In other words, it had to be something special – no, something *amazing*!

An amazing menu!

But alas, nothing came to mind. I'm not bad in the kitchen, but I'm not great, either. I like to cook modest dishes to share with friends, but nothing more. In other words, I'm a normal cook. I'm nothing exceptional, and I am definitely not a Super Chef! **How could I possibly win the contest?**

Then suddenly, I had an idea! I would make something simple, light, and above all, genuine. It would be something I could prepare by myself without asking for help from anyone. I wanted to win, but I wanted to do it the right way – on my own!

I decided to cook my **FAVOURITE** two dishes: my Mousetastic Courgette Pizza and my Fabumouse Fruit Salad with Cream.

I took off my chef's uniform, grabbed my shopping bag, and set out towards the town of Gourmetville, where I remembered seeing tons of incredible grocery stores. I was sure I would find all of the ingredients I needed to prepare my dishes.

But when I arrived in town, I was astonished. The town was deserted. All of the stores were closed – every last one!

WHAT A DISASTER!

Now where would I find the ingredients I needed? I headed back towards the castle, feeling very discouraged.

I wanted to win for my cousin and for myself, but it was impossible now.

What was I going to do?

Then suddenly, I looked up and realised there was a farm in front of me. I had passed by it on my way to Gourmetville, but in my rush, I hadn't noticed it.

There was a sign at the entrance that read:

A friendly-looking mouse with rosy cheeks stood near the gate. She was wearing an apron with flowers on it and a large straw hat.

She smiled at me.

"You look like a mouse with a problem," she said kindly. "Is it a big problem or a little one?"

"Oh!" I squeaked, surprised. "Good day, ma'am! It's true – I have a problem, and it's an **enormouse**

one! You see, I am competing in the **SUPER CHEF CONTEST**, but all the stores in Gourmetville are closed and I can't get the ingredients for my dishes!"

"Of course the stores are closed!" she replied with a laugh. "It's the final day of the Super Chef Contest. In Gourmetville, that's a city holiday. Everyone takes the day off. **But maybe I can help**."

Then she pinched my fur affectionately. **Wow, did it hurt!**

"Thank you kindly, ma'am," I replied, rubbing my cheek. "But I don't know how you could help me."

"We'll see about that!" she squeaked. Then she reached out and grabbed my shopping list. **"Give me the list! I'll figure out how to help you win the contest!"**

OPERATION MOUSETASTIC PIZZA

Aunt Mousie grasped me by the paw and pulled me onto the farm.

"Come on," she squeaked. **"We have work to do!"**

First she brought
me to the vegetable
garden. Then she
grabbed a wicker

basket and began filling it with *delicious-looking*
produce.

She dashed back and forth from one end of the
farm to another, putting more and more into the
basket. There were ripe cherry tomatoes, bunches

AND PEPPERS!

AND FRESH FRUIT!

ORGANIC FOODS are grown without the use of chemical pesticides and fertilisers, which can both be harmful to the environment. Organic farmers may use natural fertilisers such as compost or animal manure to nourish their crops. Some organic farmers use pesticides made from natural plant or animal sources to keep pests away.

Aunt Mousie's Farm

10

8

7

3

LEGEND
1. Aunt Mousie's house
2. Vegetable garden
3. Orchard
4. Vineyard
5. Barn
6. Chicken coop
7. Pigpen
8. Stables
9. Barnyard
10. Pasture
11. Dairy building

of fragrant fresh basil, three beautiful peppers, two small courgettes, and some seasonal fresh fruit she picked straight from the trees!

Next, Aunt Mousie brought me to the barn. She introduced me to her favourite cow, Margherita. Then Aunt Mousie told me to fill a pail with milk – **directly from the cow!**

Unfortunately, I am not very experienced when it comes to milking cows. To protest, first Margherita squirted me in the eye with milk. Next, she stomped on my paw. And finally, she kicked me in the tail.

OUCH! I didn't realise farm life could be so hard! But something worse was still to come ...

Next Aunt Mousie pushed me into the chicken coop and ordered me to fetch some eggs.

"You must be gentle with my chickadees, understand?" she explained. "Otherwise they will get very angry!"

I was as gentle as, well, a mouse. (I even said please!) But the hens still pecked my entire body with their sharp little beaks! **MOULDY MOZZARELLA!** Those chickens had terrible tempers!

Then Aunt Mousie pulled me into the pantry. She measured out a pound of flour and passed me a packet of natural yeast.

"Here you go!" she squeaked proudly. "It's all natural. You'll taste the goodness!"

As we filled the wicker basket, Aunt Mousie checked off the ingredients on my list.

"Got it, got it, got it!" she mumbled.

Suddenly, she gasped.

"Oh, no!" she squeaked. "We're missing the most important thing for your pizza – the mozzarella!"

She grabbed a bucket and began to beat on it with a ladle, making a tremendous racket.

DING! DING! DING! DING! DING! DING!

"Mozzarella emergency!" she squeaked at the top of her lungs.

Two rodents in white shirts came running. Then they led me to the farm's dairy building, which is where they made the most delicious cheese.

Yum … cheese!

Like all mice, I like cheese. I like fresh cheese, aged cheese, extremely aged cheese, stinky cheese, and incredibly stinky cheese. In other words, I like it all!

I just love cheese! But my favourite cheese of all is mozzarella. And there, right in front of my eyes, the two rodents made me the most enormouse piece of

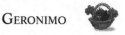

fresh, delicious mozzarella!

Yum! **I felt like the luckiest mouse in the world.**

Go Win for Me!

A short while later, I had everything I needed. It ended up being so much that the wicker basket wasn't big enough. I had to load everything into a wheelbarrow!

I thanked Aunt Mousie with all my heart.

"Thank you so much!" I told her. **"How can I ever repay you?"**

Smooch!

Thanks for everything!

"Don't worry about it," she squeaked, **kissing** me on the cheek. "Just win the contest! And when you do, be sure to tell everyone that you got your ingredients from Aunt Mousie's Farm!"

"Thank you!" I replied. "But I'm not sure I'll win. The other chefs are very good ..."

"Don't worry, you will win!" she whispered in my ear. "The secret to good cooking is in the quality of the ingredients! And I grow nothing but the best on my farm! **Go win for me!**"

Then she gave me a big push, and the wheelbarrow and I began rolling down a very steep hill.

Go win for me!

Heeeeelp!

"HEEEEEELP!" I squeaked.

Somehow, I managed to hang on to the wheelbarrow. I made it back to the castle just in the nick of time. The final round of the Super Chef Contest was about to begin! Just as I approached the castle, the wheelbarrow hit a rock and **flew** skywards, making a perfect arc through the air. **I was gripping the wheelbarrow so tightly that I went along with it !**

The wheelbarrow and I passed through an open window and landed right

Heeeeelp!

in the castle's kitchen, right in the place assigned to me, right at the moment the head judge announced the beginning of the contest!

I had made it by a whisker!

I started cooking right away, putting all of my energy into my dishes. I wanted to win, but not for myself. I wanted to win for Aunt Sweetfur, who had made Trap's delicious dishes. And for Aunt Mousie, who had been so generous!

Squeak!

So I prepared the most incredible Mousetastic Courgette Pizza I could, followed by the most Fabumouse Fruit Salad with Cream I had ever whipped up!

I knew I had done my very best, but when it was my turn to stand before the judges, my heart was in my throat. My whiskers **trembled** anxiously, and my knees were knocking from the tension.

One at a time the judges tasted my dishes.

One at a time they closed their eyes.

One at a time they licked their lips.

But no one said a word.

Then they began whispering among themselves.

The tension was almost too much to bear!

Finally, the judges all scribbled on slips of paper that they handed to the host of the competition.

"Hmmm," he mumbled solemnly. "The winner of this year's contest is Contestant Chef Number 117, Trap Stilton. I mean, it's his assistant and replacement chef – **GERONIMO STILTON!**"

After a slight pause, he continued. "Contestant Chef 117's menu was the simplest, but also the tastiest and the healthiest. The judges could tell it was prepared with genuine, fresh ingredients. Congratulations!"

I was so shocked and relieved that I fainted!

I came to a moment later when Rodento McEgo poured a ladle of **icy cold water** over my head.

"Wake up!" he squeaked at me. "You won, and now we have to give you the prize!"

A moment later, I received the famous **Great Golden Fork**. Luckily for me, my chef's hat disguised the enormouse bump on my head!

As soon as I accepted the prize, my cousin Trap arrived, using a crutch to hobble over to me, his leg in a plaster cast.

He tweaked my ear affectionately.

"Nicely done, Geronimo," he said. "You were very good, but I'm afraid I am the head chef, so ... I'll keep the **Great Golden Fork**!"

Then he **SNATCHED** the prize right out of my paw! I sighed and let him take it. I had only competed to make him happy. I wasn't interested in the prize anyway. But I was interested in repaying my debt to Aunt Mousie, and also in giving Aunt Sweetfur credit. They were the reason Trap and I had won, and I had to be sure everyone knew it.

So when the television crew from **Mousechef** began filming a moment later, I was ready.

"Dear rodent friends, I want to reveal a secret," I said, looking straight at the camera. "Everything Trap cooked was made by Aunt Sweetfur. She is the real head chef of our team. And the reason I won the **SUPER CHEF CONTEST** was because of Aunt Mousie of Aunt Mousie's Farm! She taught me that in order to cook well, you need healthy, fresh ingredients that are simple and genuine, just like those she produces at her farm!"

After that **Mousechef** broadcast, healthy cooking exploded all over Mouse Island. And back in New Mouse City, every mouse who saw me on TV suddenly

wanted to learn the recipe for my Mousetastic Pizza and Fabumouse Fruit Salad!

Who would have thought?

Life is full of surprises!

THE RODENT'S GAZETTE

1. Main entrance
2. Printing presses (where everything is printed)
3. Accounts department
4. Editorial room (where editors, illustrators, and designers work)
5. Geronimo Stilton's office
6. Geronimo's botanical garden

MAP OF NEW MOUSE CITY

1. Industrial Zone
2. Cheese Factories
3. Angorat International Airport
4. WRAT Radio and Television Station
5. Cheese Market
6. Fish Market
7. Town Hall
8. Snotnose Castle
9. The Seven Hills of Mouse Island
10. Mouse Central Station
11. Trade Centre
12. Movie Theatre
13. Gym
14. Catnegie Hall
15. Singing Stone Plaza
16. The Gouda Theatre
17. Grand Hotel
18. Mouse General Hospital
19. Botanical Gardens
20. Cheap Junk for Less (Trap's store)
21. Parking Lot
22. Museum of Modern Art
23. University and Library
24. The Daily Rat
25. The Rodent's Gazette
26. Trap's House
27. Fashion District
28. The Mouse House Restaurant
29. Environmental Protection Centre
30. Harbour Office
31. Mousidon Square Garden
32. Golf Course
33. Swimming Pool
34. Blushing Meadow Tennis Courts
35. Curlyfur Island Amusement Park
36. Geronimo's House
37. Historic District
38. Public Library
39. Shipyard
40. Thea's House
41. New Mouse Harbour
42. Luna Lighthouse
43. The Statue of Liberty
44. Hercule Poirat's Office
45. Petunia Pretty Paws's House
46. Grandfather William's House

MAP OF MOUSE ISLAND

1. Big Ice Lake
2. Frozen Fur Peak
3. Slipperyslopes Glacier
4. Coldcreeps Peak
5. Ratzikistan
6. Transratania
7. Mount Vamp
8. Roastedrat Volcano
9. Brimstone Lake
10. Poopedcat Pass
11. Stinko Peak
12. Dark Forest
13. Vain Vampires Valley
14. Goosebumps Gorge
15. The Shadow Line Pass
16. Penny-Pincher Castle
17. Nature Reserve Park
18. Las Ratayas Marinas
19. Fossil Forest
20. Lake Lake
21. Lake Lakelake
22. Lake Lakelakelake
23. Cheddar Crag
24. Cannycat Castle
25. Valley of the Giant Sequoia
26. Cheddar Springs
27. Sulphurous Swamp
28. Old Reliable Geyser
29. Vole Vale
30. Ravingrat Ravine
31. Gnat Marshes
32. Munster Highlands
33. Mousehara Desert
34. Oasis of the Sweaty Camel
35. Cabbagehead Hill
36. Rattytrap Jungle
37. Rio Mosquito
38. Mousefort Beach
39. San Mouscisco
40. Swissville
41. Cheddarton
42. Mouseport
43. New Mouse City
44. Pirate Ship of Cats

THE COLLECTION

HAVE YOU READ ALL OF GERONIMO'S ADVENTURES?

ABOUT THE AUTHOR

Born in New Mouse City, Mouse Island, GERONIMO STILTON is Rattus Emeritus of Mousomorphic Literature and of Neo-Ratonic Comparative Philosophy. For the past twenty years, he has been running The Rodent's Gazette, New Mouse City's most widely read daily newspaper.

Stilton was awarded the Ratitzer Prize for his scoops on *The Curse of the Cheese Pyramid* and *The Search for Sunken Treasure*. He has also received the Andersen Prize

for Personality of the Year. His works have been published all over the globe.

In his spare time, Mr. Stilton collects antique cheese rinds and plays golf. But what he most enjoys is telling stories to his nephew Benjamin.